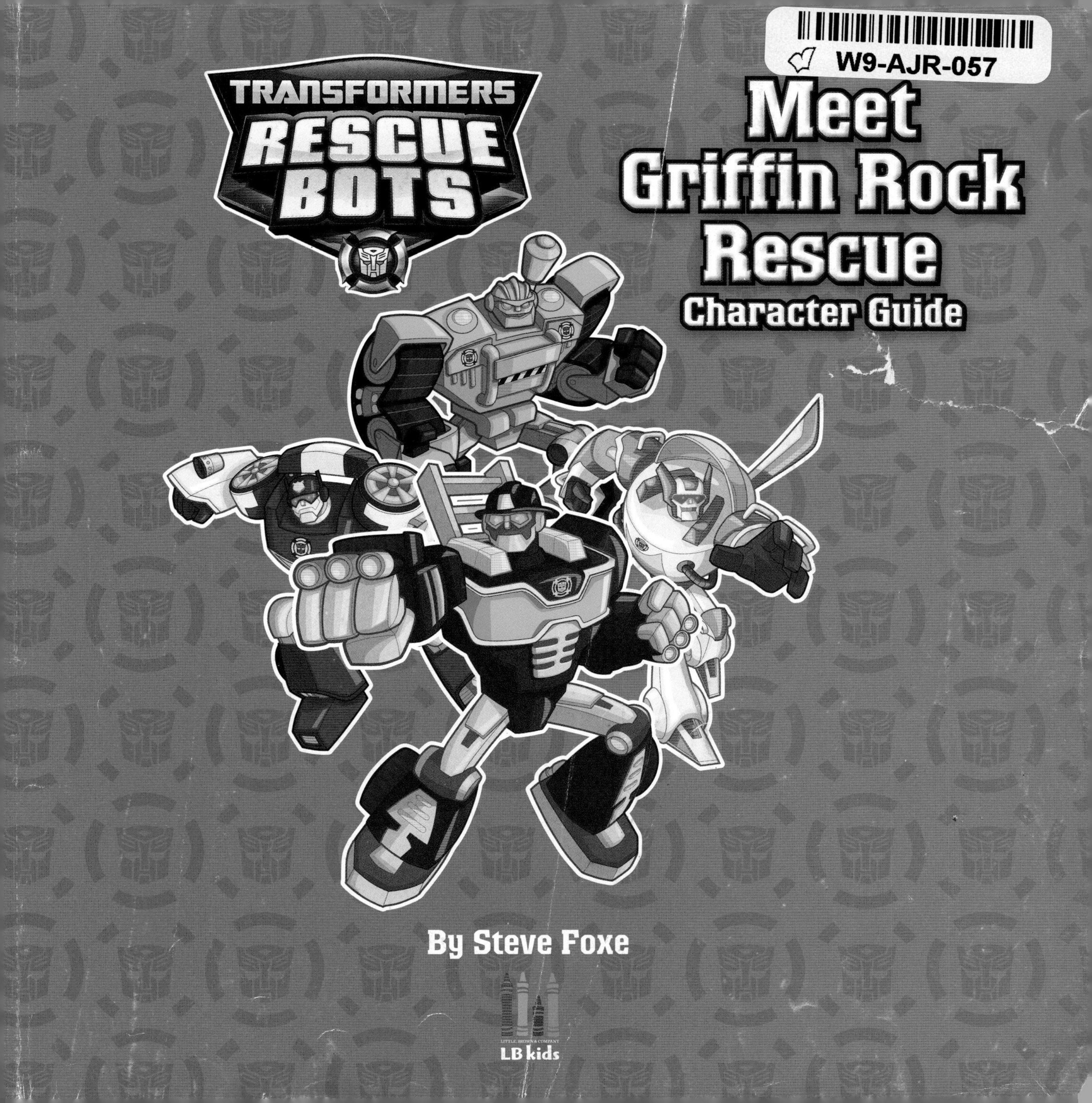
TRANSFORMERS
RESCUE
BOTS
Meet
Griffin Rock
Rescue
Character Guide
By Steve Foxe
LITTLE, BROWN & COMPANY
LB kids

Little, Brown and Company

Hachette Book Group
1290 Avenue of the Americas, New York, NY 10104
Visit us at lb-kids.com

LB kids is an imprint of Little, Brown and Company.
The LB kids name and logo are trademarks of Hachette Book Group, Inc.

The publisher is not responsible for websites (or their content) that are not owned by the publisher.

First Edition: June 2016

Library of Congress Control Number: 2015949307

ISBN 978-0-316-38978-5

10 9 8 7 6 5 4 3 2 1

APS

Printed in China

Licensed By:

The Rescue Bots are a special group of Transformers sworn to serve and protect the human race. The first Rescue Bots were part of Rescue Force Sigma-17. Their spaceship drifted through space until Optimus Prime called them to Earth. The Autobot leader ordered the Rescue Bots to live and work with a human family on the island of Griffin Rock, Maine. They all help keep the planet safe!

The town of Griffin Rock is home to many scientists who test strange, new gadgets on the island. Though most of these experiments eventually benefit all humankind, some do go awry. Good thing the Rescue Bots are always on call!

RESCUE HEADQUARTERS

The Rescue Bots and their human partners detect these disasters from Rescue Headquarters, Griffin Rock's fire station. Whenever trouble pops up, the Rescue Bots best suited for each mission are deployed. Sometimes all the Rescue Bots must roll to the rescue!

Heatwave

Heatwave the Fire-Bot is the leader of the Rescue Bots. He can change into a big red fire truck, a speedy fireboat, and a brachiosaurus Dino Bot. No flame is too hot for Heatwave's water cannons!

At first, Heatwave did not want to work with the humans on Earth. Now he is proud to partner with firefighter Kade Burns and help the rest of his team keep Griffin Rock safe.

Chase

Chase the Police-Bot loves following the law. He was the first Bot from Rescue Force Sigma-17 to embrace living on Earth. His vehicle mode is a police cruiser with flashing lights and a loud siren.

Chase can also change into a stegosaurus Dino Bot with a spiky tail. He works with Chief Charlie Burns, the human leader of the Rescue Team. Together, they can hunt down any criminal and help stop any disaster.

Boulder

Boulder the Construction-Bot is a gentle giant. He loves Earth culture and fluffy animals. When Boulder needs to protect his human friends, he changes into a powerful bulldozer or a strong triceratops Dino Bot.

Boulder is also Rescue Force Sigma-17's best engineer. His human teammate is Graham Burns. Together, their mechanical knowledge helps fix damaged or malfunctioning technology on Griffin Rock.

Blades

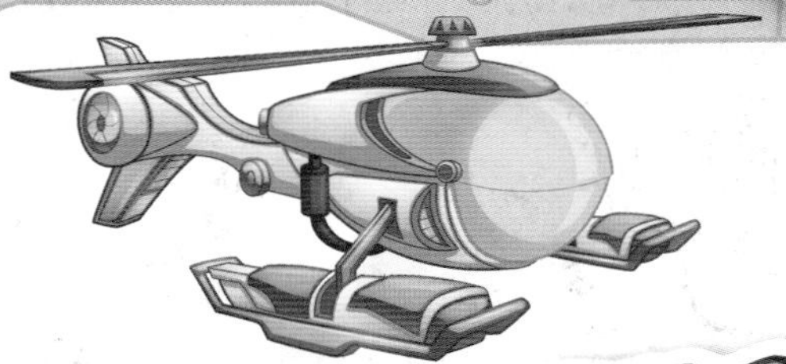

Blades the Copter-Bot is the youngest member of the Rescue Bots. He had to overcome his fear of heights to fly in his helicopter mode. Now he can soar through the air as a pterodactyl Dino Bot, too!

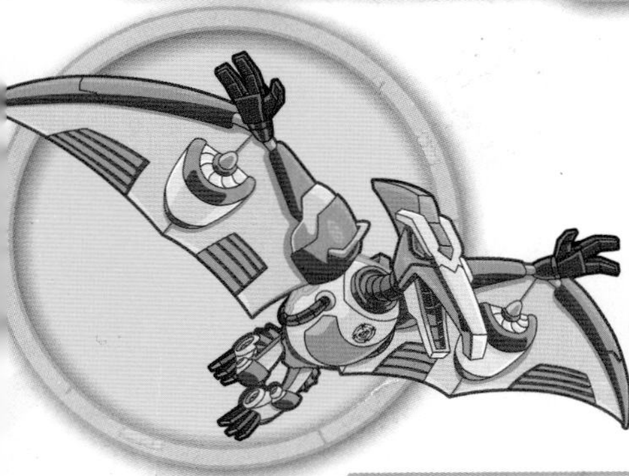

Blades may be afraid of heights, but his human partner, Dani Burns, is not. Dani's ace piloting skills keep Blades calm under pressure. Together, they protect the skies over Griffin Rock.

Bumblebee

Bumblebee is one of Optimus Prime's most trusted Autobot allies. He lost his voice during the War for Cybertron and can only speak in beeps and whistles. Bumblebee changes into a yellow sports car with black racing stripes and a raptor Dino Bot.

Bumblebee first met the Rescue Bots when he tracked a meteorite to nearby Wayward Island. Optimus asked him to spend some time with the team. Now Bumblebee assists the Rescue Bots whenever they need him!

Optimus Prime

Optimus Prime is the heroic leader of the Autobots. He holds the Matrix of Leadership, an object of great power. Optimus gave the Rescue Bots a mission to live on Earth and protect humans from natural disasters and science gone wrong.

Optimus changes into a blue-and-red semitruck. On a mission to the mysterious Wayward Island, Optimus also gained the ability to change into a mighty Tyrannosaurus rex by scanning Trex, Doc Greene's dinosaur robot!

High Tide

High Tide is a drill instructor with a cranky attitude, but he is one of Optimus Prime's oldest friends. High Tide changes into a submarine to assist with water rescues. If needed, he can also combine with his ship to form a giant Mega-Bot.

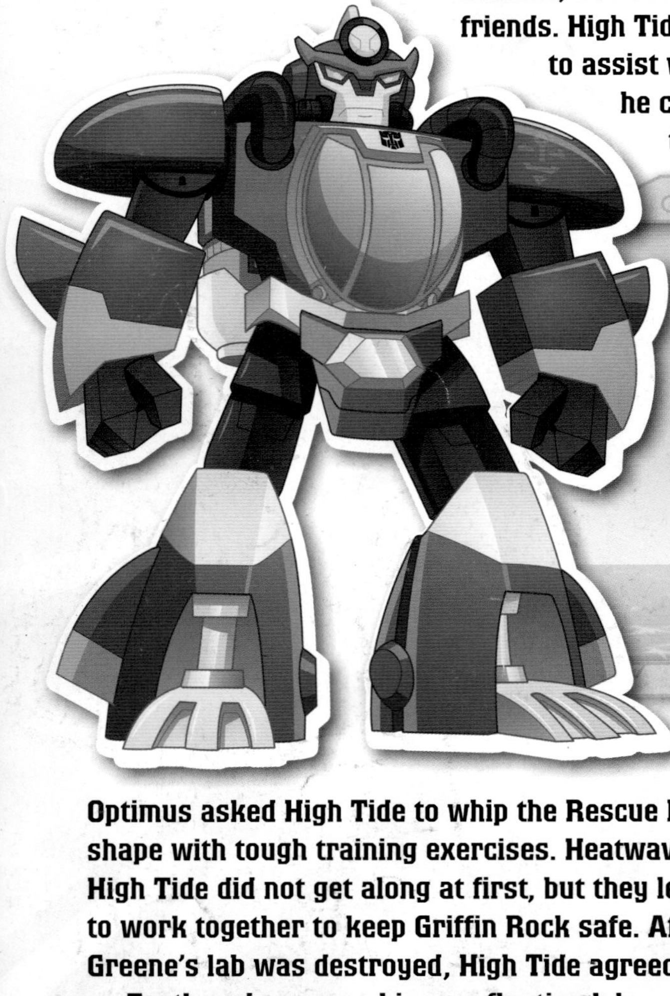

Optimus asked High Tide to whip the Rescue Bots into shape with tough training exercises. Heatwave and High Tide did not get along at first, but they learned to work together to keep Griffin Rock safe. After Doc Greene's lab was destroyed, High Tide agreed to remain on Earth and serve as his new floating lab.

Blurr

Blurr and his partner, Salvage, crashed onto Earth thousands of years ago during a meteor shower. They slept in stasis until the Rescue Bots found them. Blurr is a purple Autobot who changes into a lightning-fast race car.

Blurr has trouble following orders on Earth. He just wants to race! He even stole the Rescue Bots' spaceship to escape the planet, but he returned it and saved the day in the process. Optimus Prime later gave Blurr and Salvage a mission to start their own Rescue Team away from Griffin Rock.

Salvage

Salvage is very different from his companion, Blurr. Where Blurr can be edgy and impatient, Salvage is quiet and calm. He changes into a big green garbage truck and likes to recycle trash and turn forgotten objects into effective rescue tools.

When Blurr stole the Rescue Bots' spaceship to leave Earth, Salvage talked him into returning it. Optimus Prime rewarded Salvage by making him a Rescue Bot. Salvage joined Blurr to lead their own Rescue Bot squad elsewhere.

Trex & Servo

Trex is a Tyrannosaurus rex robot that Doc Greene programmed to guard his lab. When he's not scaring away intruders, Trex makes coffee for his master. Trex has been hacked and forced to turn against the Rescue Bots in the past, but Doc Greene always fixes him. On a mission to Wayward Island, Trex once saved Doc Greene from being crushed by falling rocks.

Servo is High Tide's faithful dog robot. He can change into all sorts of useful things, like a crowbar or a wheelbarrow, and can even be commanded with a dog whistle. When he's not working with the Rescue Bots, Servo enjoys playing fetch with Cody Burns or chasing Mayor Luskey's wife's dog, Poopsie, around Griffin Rock.

Charlie Burns & Cody Burns

Chief Charlie Burns is the human leader of the Rescue Team and the father of Kade, Graham, Dani, and Cody. His Rescue Bot partner is Chase the Police-Bot. Chief Burns uses his rescue tools and years of experience to assist the Bots!

Cody Burns is the youngest member of the Burns clan. Though Cody often serves as the Rescue Team's dispatcher, he wants to be out in the field with his family someday and often finds himself falling into dangerous rescue missions by accident. Cody is best friends with Doc Greene's daughter, Frankie. He plays with Servo and always encourages teamwork.

Kade Burns & Dani Burns

Kade Burns is a firefighter and the oldest Burns sibling. He has a quick temper and often clashes with his Rescue Bot partner, Heatwave. He loves his family, even if he is sometimes a bit mean to his little brother Cody.

Danielle "Dani" Burns is the thrill-seeking daughter of Chief Charlie Burns. Her Rescue Bot partner, Blades, does not like heights, but Dani's piloting skills keep the Copter-Bot in the air, conquering his fears.

Graham Burns & Woody Burns

Graham Burns loves science and engineering. He lets his siblings Dani and Kade handle most of the action, but he contributes to the team by being the brains behind many missions alongside his partner, Boulder.

Woodrow "Woody" Burns is the younger brother of Chief Burns. Woody is a free spirit and spends his time chasing aliens and the unknown. Though he's a little spacey, when his family needs help, Woody is always ready to pitch in with his own kind of heroics!

Doc Greene & Frankie Greene

Doc Greene is an eccentric but brilliant scientist who lives in Griffin Rock. His experiments sometimes backfire and cause trouble around the island, keeping the Rescue Bots very busy. The dinosaur robot Trex and the floating helper robot Dither are two of Doc Greene's many inventions. After working together on lots of scientific endeavors, Doc Greene married Professor Baranova.

Francine "Frankie" Greene is Doc Greene's equally brilliant and brave daughter. She is best friends with Cody Burns and likes to accompany the Rescue Bots on missions. She wants to be a scientist like her father and often helps clean up his mistakes.

Mayor Luskey & Huxley Prescott

Mayor Luskey has been the mayor of Griffin Rock for many years. He is married to a former winner of the Miss Griffin Rock pageant who has a tiny dog named Poopsie that gets into all sorts of trouble. Mayor Luskey is quick to take credit for good ideas and blame others for bad ones.

Huxley Prescott will do anything to get the scoop. This journalist and TV reporter never goes anywhere without a microphone and his floating camera. Huxley believes aliens exist on Earth, which means he is always ready to report when the Rescue Bots leap into action!

Dr. Thaddeus Morocco

Dr. Thaddeus Morocco is a long-lived evil genius who menaces the Rescue Bots. He became friends and science partners with the famous author Jules Verne in 1862. Verne shared his "Verne Device" with Dr. Morocco, who used it to extend his life and travel through time.

Dr. Morocco commands a personal army of MorBots. MorBots are shape-shifting robots with cannon arms, rocket boots, and an armored tank mode. Dr. Morocco once traveled back in time and took control of Griffin Rock using his MorBots. Luckily, the Rescue Bots defeated him and reset the timeline.

Madeline Pynch and Priscilla Pynch & Myles and Evan

Madeline Pynch is a rich businesswoman who values money over people and the environment. She wants to drill for oil and mine for gold under Griffin Rock. She once teamed up with Dr. Morocco to force the Rescue Bots to work for her!

Madeline's spoiled daughter, Priscilla Pynch, uses her mother's money to buy her way through life and bully her classmates Cody Burns and Frankie Greene. At least she was somewhat thankful when the Rescue Bots saved her from the ravenous plants in the Sky Forest.

Griffin Rock's resident thieves are two brothers named Myles and Evan. Myles is a talented hacker. He uses his skills to break into the science labs on the island. Evan rarely speaks, but when he does, it is usually in grunts. No matter what schemes they plan, the Rescue Bots are always around to return the stolen goods and enforce the law!

Colonel Quint Quarry & Vigil

Colonel Quint Quarry is a hi-tech hunter who uses advanced tools to catch his prey. He owns the Quarry Safariland, his "playground" off the coast of Maine. When Optimus Prime turned into a feral Dino Bot, Colonel Quarry captured the Autobot leader and set him free in Safariland to practice his hunting skills. The Rescue Bots cured Optimus and helped Chief Burns arrest Colonel Quarry!

When Griffin Rock's main computer crashed, Mayor Luskey brought in the supercomputer Vigil to take over. Despite Doc Greene's warnings, Mayor Luskey gave Vigil full control of the island. Vigil overstepped its primary directive and took the whole town prisoner! Cody Burns saved everyone by tricking Vigil into frying its own systems.

SERVE & PROTECT

A routine patrol with four Bots in stasis,
Years later awoke in the strangest of places.
Earth was their home now and in addition,
Optimus Prime gave them this mission:

"Learn from the humans, serve and protect,
Live in their world, earn their respect.
A family of heroes will be your allies,
To others remain robots in disguise."

Rescue Bots, roll to the rescue,
Humans in need, heroes indeed.
Rescue Bots, roll to the rescue, Rescue Bots.

With Cody to guide them and show them the way,
Rescue Bots will be saving the day.

Rescue Bots, roll to the rescue,
Rescue Bots.